D1500371

About This Book

From the snowy, wintery window of her art studio, Dahlov Ipcar sees a wild and wondrous world.

With vivid imagination and vibrant colors, she has captured a lively part of the Christmas season at her farm in Maine. From one shining star that graces the top of her living outdoor tree, she envisions many captivating creatures of the field and forest who come to visit.

From young black bears to snowy owls, from evening grosbeaks to happy chipmunks, this book presents a lively panorama of the wild creatures Dahlov Ipcar has seen and enjoyed.

A holiday classic, *My Wonderful Christmas Tree* beautifully conveys the feeling of the Christmas season outdoors in New England.

This Book
Belongs To

_____

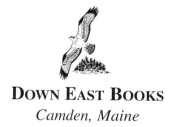

DOWN EAST BOOKS
Camden, Maine

MY
WONDERFUL

CHRISTMAS TREE

by DAHLOV IPCAR

DOWN EAST BOOKS

Printed by Oceanic Graphic Printing, Inc., Hong Kong
Down East Books; P.O. Box 679; Camden, ME 04843 • BOOK ORDERS: 1-800-685-7962

4 2 5 3 1

Library of Congress Cataloging-in-Publication Data

Ipcar, Dahlov Zorach, 1917–
     My wonderful Christmas tree / by Dahlov Ipcar.
         p.   cm.
     Summary: Looking out her window on Christmas Eve, the author
introduces the numbers from one to twelve as she spies several
animals nestled in the boughs of an evergreen tree.
     ISBN 0-89272-475-7
     [1. Counting. 2. Animals Fiction. 3. Christmas Fiction.
4. Stories in rhyme.] I. Title
PZ8.3.I63My   1999
[E]—dc21   99-37003
                                                 CIP

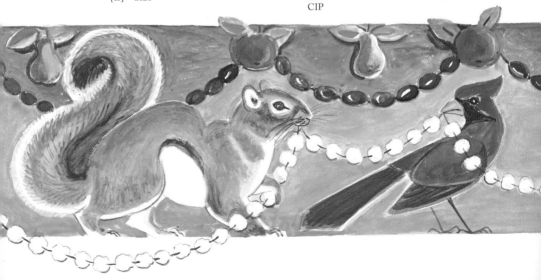

Dedicated to my granddaughter,
Katie Lauren Ipcar

I looked out my window
On Christmas night,
And there I saw
A most wonderful sight —
One shining star,
One brilliant light,
Sparkling, glimmering,
Gleaming bright,
High in my tree
On Christmas night,
One shining star.

I looked out my window
On Christmas night,
And there I saw
A most wonderful sight —
Two black bears,
Velvety black
Soft and warm
Clinging together
Against the storm,
Hugging each other
Close and tight
In a starlit tree
On Christmas night,
Two black bears.

I saw three bobcats.
Three bobcats with spotted coats,
Tufted ears, and soft white throats,
Crouching there in their treetop lair.

Wide awake, their gold eyes shine
High in the boughs of the dark green pine.
Softly purring, whiskers stirring,
Three bobcats.

I saw four porcupines.
Round black pincushions spiked with spines,
Prickled and stickled all around,
Fat and happy, and safe and sound.

In the dark tree where they like to dine
On shiny, spiny needles of pine,
A Christmas dinner that tastes just fine
To four porcupines.

I saw five raccoons.
Bold little bandits with neat black masks,
Clean white hands, and clean white feet.
They wash their food before they eat.

Living high in the tall green tree;
This is the place they like to be,
Living high near the stars and moon,
Five raccoons.

I saw six snowy owls,
Soft and white as a drift of snow,
Spreading their wings
To the winds that blow,

Round eyes gleaming like coins of gold,
Never minding the winter cold,
Never minding the wind that howls,
Six snowy owls.

I saw seven ruffed grouse,
High in my tree on Christmas eve,
Looking like clumps of autumn leaves,
Roosting high in the sighing boughs,

This is their own green-growing house.
Dreaming dreams of Christmas morn,
Of partridge berries and golden corn,
Seven ruffed grouse.

I saw eight gray squirrels,
Small feet frisking, soft tails whisking,
Leaping and rippling through the tree,
Dancing a dance so light and free.

Twirling, swirling
Like falling leaves,
High in my tree on Christmas eve,
Eight gray squirrels.

I saw nine bluejays,
Bright and blue as a winter day,
Spreading their tails like Chinese fans,
Sounding blue notes from their white throats,

Screeching high shrieks
From their black beaks,
Sassy shrill squawks, that's how jays talk,
Nine bluejays.

I saw ten evening grosbeaks,
Gold and silver shining bright
Like ornaments in candlelight,
Singing songs in my Christmas tree,

Singing songs for Christmas eve,
Songs of moon and stars and night,
Snowflakes falling soft and white,
Ten evening grosbeaks.

I saw eleven chipmunks
Stuffing their cheeks with happy squeeks.
Gathering pinenuts rich and sweet,
That's a chipmunk's Christmas treat.

And running up and down their backs,
Black and white stripes
Like railroad tracks,
Eleven chipmunks.

I saw twelve chickadees
Dressed so neatly in white and gray
Like ice and snow on a winter day.
All their black caps fitting tight
To keep them warm on Christmas night.

And they sang their song to me
In my wonderful Christmas tree,
"Chick-a-dee-dee-dee-dee-dee."
Merry Christmas to you and me!
Twelve chickadees.

Twelve chickadees,
Eleven chipmunks,
Ten evening grosbeaks,
Nine bluejays,
Eight gray squirrels,
Seven ruffed grouse,
Six snowy owls,
Five raccoons,
Four porcupines,
Three bobcats,
Two black bears,
One shining star.

One shining star,

Two black bears,

Three bobcats,

Four porcupines,

Five raccoons,

Six snowy owls,

Seven ruffed grouse,

Eight gray squirrels,

Nine bluejays,

Ten evening grosbeaks,

Eleven chipmunks,

Twelve chickadees . . .

All in my
Wonderful
Christmas
Tree.

About the Author/Artist

Dahlov Ipcar lives year round on the farm near Bath, Maine, where she and her husband raised their two sons. Mrs. Ipcar has written and illustrated more than thirty picture books for children, among them *A Flood of Creatures, Lobsterman,* and *Lost and Found.*

The author has had a lifelong career as an artist. Her parents, William and Marguerite Zorach, were both artists, and they encouraged her from earliest childhood to express herself creatively in both art and writing. She has had many shows of her own in New York City and even more in Maine. Her work is in the permanent collections of several museums, including the Metropolitan Museum of Art and the Whitney Museum of American Art.